TWO DUMB DUCKS

by

MAXWELL EATON III

Alfred A. Knopf 🦆 New York

Steve and Carl are ducks.

They do not like seagulls.
Seagulls call them . . .

They try telling the seagulls to stop.

They even try to look smarter.

But seagulls still call them . . .

Steve and Carl get MAD!

Steve and Carl get ANGRY!

Steve and Carl get EVEN....

That night they sneak across the pond to search for the sleeping seagulls.

They search.

And they search.

And they search.

But after wandering all night,
they fall asleep . . .

Yet Steve and Carl are not mad.

Steve and Carl are not angry.

The seagulls dive behind a rock.

What are they afraid of?

They think Steve and Carl are monsters!

But Steve and Carl are ducks.

Steve likes cans.

Carl likes socks.

Sometimes they like to play Muck Monsters.